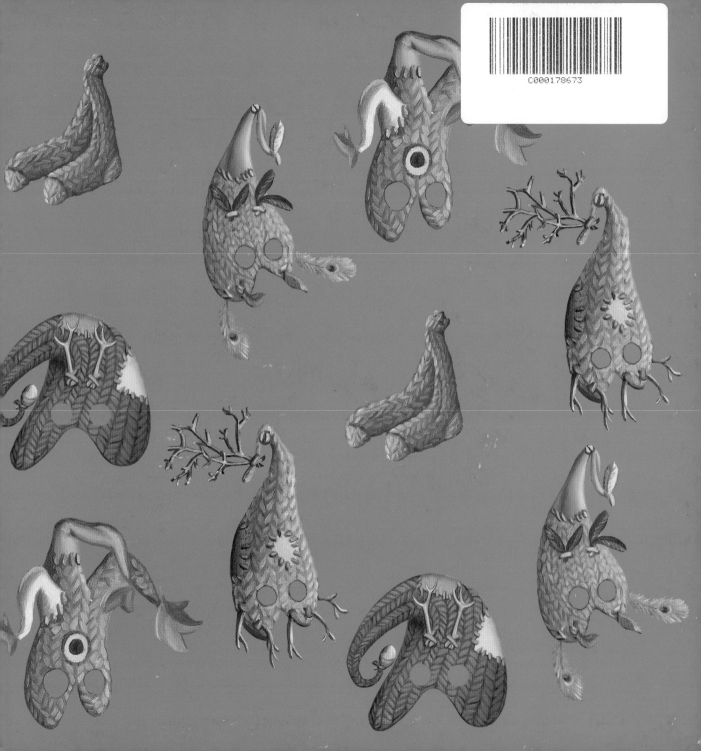

In the deep, deep darkness

Of the deep dark wood,

Lives a hairy Snafferpickle

In a Snafferpickle hood.

In the deep, deep darkness

Of his deep dark cave,

He wears the Snafferpickle hoods

That his grandma gave.

In the deep, deep darkness

Past the deep dark trees,

The Snafferpickle sits

Watching everything he sees.

In the deep, deep darkness

By the deep dark river,

The Snafferpickle lurks

And makes your insides shiver!

In the deep, deep darkness

You'd better watch out...

Here comes the Snafferpickle

So get ready to SHOUT!

The Snafferpickle's seen us...

That's not so good.

In the deep, deep darkness

Of the deep dark wood.

In the deep, deep darkness

Where things go "Boo"!

The Snafferpickle's here,

And he's going to EAT YOU!

But goodness me, Snafferpickle

What were we thinking?

You're not that scary

Not even worth blinking!

You don't scare us

In your deep dark wood.

But we scared you

LIKE CHILDREN SHOULD!

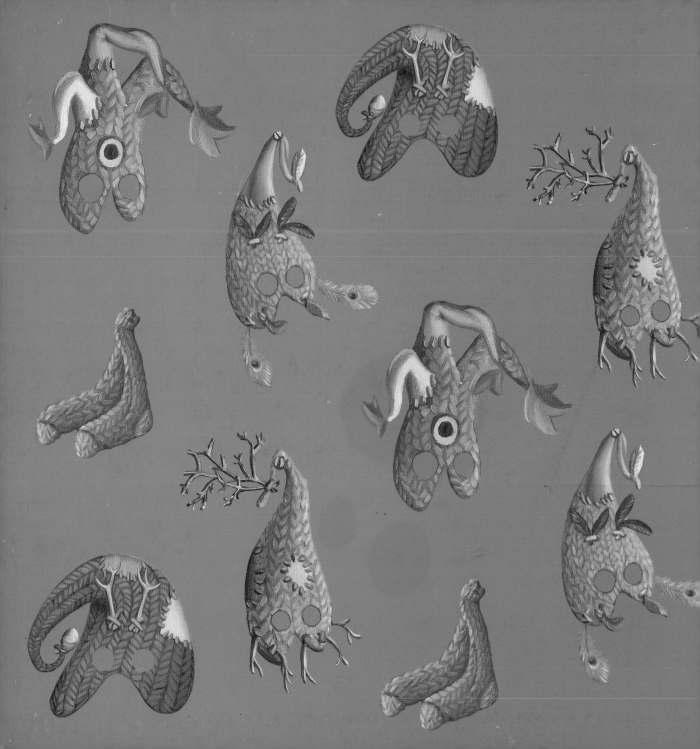